Licensed exclusively to Top That Publishing Ltd
Tide Mill Way, Woodbridge, Suffolk, IP12 1AP, UK
www.topthatpublishing.com
Copyright © 2018 Tide Mill Media
All rights reserved
0 2 4 6 8 9 7 5 3 1
Manufactured in China

Written by Nat Lambert
Illustrated by Rosie Butcher

ISBN 978-1-78700-590-7

Little Red Riding Hood

Written by Nat Lambert
Illustrated by Rosie Butcher

Once upon a time, there was a girl called
Little Red Riding Hood, who lived at the edge of
a big, dark forest. Little Red Riding Hood had a
grandmother, who lived on her own in a cottage
on the other side of the forest.

One morning, Little Red Riding Hood set off to visit her
grandmother for lunch, as she did every week.

Little Red Riding Hood skipped along the path through the forest, but soon she became tired and stopped to rest under a tree.

As she closed her eyes, Little Red Riding Hood
heard a voice behind her.

'Hello, little girl. Are you lost?'

'I'm not lost. I'm going to visit my grandmother, who lives in a cottage on the other side of the forest,' Little Red Riding Hood replied.

What Little Red Riding Hood didn't know was that she was talking to a big bad wolf!

The big bad wolf wanted to gobble up
Little Red Riding Hood right then,
but he decided he would race ahead
to her grandmother's cottage so
he could gobble them both up for lunch!

The wolf ran ahead until he reached Little Red Riding Hood's grandmother's cottage.
He knocked on the door and listened.

Knock, knock!

'Who's there?' called a voice from inside.

'It's me, Little Red Riding Hood,' replied the wolf.

The wolf opened the door and before Little Red Riding Hood's grandmother could even scream, he gobbled her right up!

Quickly, the wolf put on her nightcap
and glasses and tucked himself up in bed.

When Little Red Riding Hood reached her grandmother's cottage, she knocked on the door and called out,

'Grandmother, it's me,
Little Red Riding Hood.'

'Come in,' said a voice from inside the cottage. So, Little Red Riding Hood opened the door and went inside.

Little Red Riding Hood thought that her grandmother looked a little strange, so she switched on a lamp near the bed.

'**Grandmother, what big eyes you have!**'
exclaimed Little Red Riding Hood.

'**All the better to see you with, my dear,**'
replied the wolf.

Little Red Riding Hood crept a little closer.

'Grandmother, what big ears you have!' gasped Little Red Riding Hood.

'All the better to hear you with, my dear,' replied the wolf.

Little Red Riding Hood crept right up to the bed.

'Grandmother, what big teeth you have!'
cried Little Red Riding Hood, as the light glinted off the wolf's teeth.

'All the better to eat you with my dear!'
shouted the wolf, leaping out of bed.

Little Red Riding Hood screamed
and swung her basket as hard as she
could at the big bad wolf.

The basket was very heavy and
it knocked the wolf right over.

Just then, the door to the cottage swung open and Little Red Riding Hood's father arrived, on his way home from woodchopping.

Little Red Riding Hood told her father all about the big bad wolf and how he had eaten her grandmother and tried to eat her too!

Little Red Riding Hood's father grabbed the wolf, squeezed his tummy… and out popped Little Red Riding Hood's grandmother!

Little Red Riding Hood's grandmother was very happy
to be back and she agreed to come for tea at Little
Red Riding Hood's house. Little Red Riding
Hood, her grandmother, and her father
walked out of the cottage and pulled
the door closed behind them.

And they never saw the big bad wolf again. The End.